One Rainy Day

One Rainy Day

by Tammi Salzano   Illustrated by Hannah Wood

SCHOLASTIC INC.
New York Toronto London Auckland
Sydney Mexico City New Delhi Hong Kong

Duck loves the rain.

One rainy day means...

red boots

an orange umbrella

a green frog

blue puddles

pink worms

black bugs

a brown mud pie

white boats

yellow flowers

and a purple towel
from Mama Duck!

Duck loves rainy days!

For John, Alex, and Julianna,
the brightest colors in my world
-T.S.

To Vicky, my mummy duck
-H.W.

ISBN 978-0-545-34126-4

Text copyright © 2011 by Tammi Salzano.
Illustrations copyright © 2011 by Hannah Wood. All rights reserved.
Published by Scholastic Inc., 557 Broadway, New York, NY 10012, by arrangement
with Tiger Tales, an imprint of ME Media, LLC. SCHOLASTIC and associated logos
are trademarks and/or registered trademarks of Scholastic Inc.

12 11 10 9 8 7 6   11 12 13 14 15 16/0

Printed in the U.S.A.   40

First Scholastic printing, April 2011